A Perfect Picnic

Logansport-Cass County Public Library

By Sarah Albee

Illustrated by Tom Brannon

A Random House PICTUREBACK® Book

Random House 🏠 New York

Copyright © 2003 Sesame Workshop. All rights reserved under International and Pan-American Copyright Conventions.
Published in the United States by Random House Children's Books, a division of Random House, Inc., New York,
and simultaneously in Canada by Random House of Canada Limited, Toronto, in conjunction with Sesame Workshop.
Sesame Street, Sesame Workshop, and their logos are trademarks and service marks of Sesame Workshop.

Library of Congress Control Number: 2001088372
ISBN: 0-375-81455-8
www.randomhouse.com/kids/sesame
www.sesamestreet.com
Printed in the United States of America 10 9 8 7 6 5 4 3 2 1
PICTUREBACK, RANDOM HOUSE, and the Random House colophon are registered trademarks and the
Please Read to Me colophon is a trademark of Random House, Inc.

"It's a perfect day for a picnic!" said Bert.
"What a fine way to celebrate spring.
Smell those spring flowers! See the lambs in the field!
Feel that breeze! Hear those cute birdies sing!"

"Look!" Ernie said. "There's a baseball game!"
Elmo said, "And a bicycle race!"
"Ah, springtime," said Bert as he set down the basket.
"This looks like a nice, quiet place."

Zoe brought over some flowers.
It was then that Bert started to sneeze.
"Achoo!" said Bert. "All these spring blossoms . . .
ACHOO . . . give me . . . *COUGH* . . . allergies."

The gentle spring breeze began to pick up.
It blew away Zoe's bouquet,
And then all the napkins, the spoons, Ernie's hat . . .
Why, that wind nearly blew Bert away!

Just then the food started marching.
Away went the bread and the jam.
"The ANTS," Bert cried, "are taking the food!
They just marched away with the ham!"

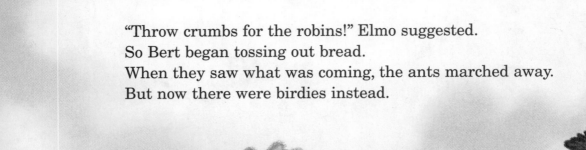

"Throw crumbs for the robins!" Elmo suggested.
So Bert began tossing out bread.
When they saw what was coming, the ants marched away.
But now there were birdies instead.

"This is *not* how I'd planned things!" Bert said with a sigh
As chipmunks made off with his carrot.

A lamb ate some lettuce straight from Elmo's sandwich!
But Elmo was happy to share it.

CRACK! went a bat as it hit a baseball.
They all looked up at the sky.
That baseball came whizzing and hit with a SPLAT!
Smack in the chocolate cream pie.

"Here come the racers!" Zoe announced.
"Look out, Bert! They're headed toward you!"
ZOOM! All the bicycles sped through a puddle,
Splashing Bert top to bottom with goo.

"Well, at least there's no rain on our spring celebration,"
Said Bert with another small sigh.
"Uh-oh." Ernie pointed as gray clouds rushed in.
Then raindrops poured down from the sky.

"Our spring picnic is ruined!" the others said sadly.
"The rainstorm has spoiled *everything*!"
Bert smiled just a little. "Now cheer up," he said.
"Without rain . . ."

"... it just wouldn't be spring!"